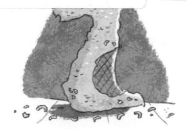

THE BINDER OF DOOM

HYDRANT-HYDRA

by Troy Cummings

BRANCHES

SCHOLASTIC INC.

READ MORE BOOKS IN THE BINDER OF DOOM SERIES!

1

2

3

4

HAVE YOU READ ALL OF THE NOTEBOOK OF DOOM BOOKS?

1

2

3

4

5

6

7

8

9

10

11

12

13

SPECIAL EDITION

COLLECT THEM ALL!

SCHOLASTIC.COM/DOOM

TABLE OF CONTENTS

To Carson, the coolest reader in Canada!

Library of Congress Cataloging-in-Publication Data

Names: Cummings, Troy, author, illustrator. | Cummings, Troy. Binder of doom ; 4.

Title: Hydrant-hydra / Troy Cummings.

Description: First edition. | New York : Branches/Scholastic, 2020. | Series: The Binder of Doom; 4 | Audience: Ages 6-8. | Audience: Grades 2-3. |

Summary: It has been a busy summer of makerspace projects at the library and monster hunting for the three members of the Super Secret Monster Patrol, and the puddles that are appearing all over town are a clue to the identity of another monster – an angry hydra water monster who is obsessed with cleaning up (literally) the town of Stermont, even if it means drowning all the messy children who live there.

Identifiers: LCCN 2019044815 | ISBN 9781338314762 (paperback) | ISBN 9781338314779 (library binding)

Subjects: LCSH: Monsters – Juvenile fiction. | Makerspaces in libraries – Juvenile fiction. | Public libraries – Juvenile fiction. | Best friends – Juvenile fiction. | Horror tales. | CYAC: Monsters – Fiction. | Makerspaces – Fiction. | Libraries – Fiction. | Best friends – Fiction. | Friendship – Fiction. | Horror stories. | LCGFT: Horror fiction.

Classification: LCC PZ7.C91494 Hy 2020 | DDC 813.6 [Fic] – dc23 LC record available at https://lccn.loc.gov/2019044815

10 9 8 7 6 5 4 3 2 1   20 21 22 23 24

Printed in China   62

First edition, July 2020

Edited by Katie Carella

Book design by Troy Cummings and Sarah Dvojack

CHAPTER 1

SWAMP CREATURES

"**H**elp!" said Alexander's dad as he opened the door. "Swamp creatures are taking over my house!"

Glops of mud fell from Alexander's shoes as he clomped up the front steps.

His friends Rip and Nikki followed — they were even muddier.

"**GRAWRR!**" they said as they held out their muddy fingers like monster claws.

1

Then Rip and Nikki laughed.

But not Alexander. He never joked about monsters. He knew that monsters were real. And Stermont was crawling with them!

Alexander's dad smiled as he looked across the yard. "I see muddy trucks, muddy footprints, and a dozen mud pies," he said. "Looks like you mud-monsters had fun today!"

Alexander winked at Rip and Nikki. His dad didn't know it, but his two best friends were secretly monsters — good monsters!

NIKKI: A jampire. Eats red, juicy food, sees in the dark, has fangs, and avoids sunlight.

RIP: Seems like an ordinary boy. But when he eats sweets, he transforms into a knuckle-fisted punch-smasher.

Rip keeps monster-ants in his pocket. When they eat sweets, they transform into gi-norm-ants.

Together, Alexander, Rip, and Nikki were members of the Super Secret Monster Patrol. The S.S.M.P. protected Stermont from all sorts of stomping, roaring, kid-eating monsters.

"Okay, Al — shower time!" said Alexander's dad. "Say good night to your friends."

"Bye, Salamander!" said Rip and Nikki.

Alexander smiled. Salamander was his nickname.

He plopped off his muddy shoes and headed inside.

"Seriously, kiddo!" said his dad. "You find new ways to get messy every day!"

"It just means I'm having a good summer!" said Alexander. He high-fived his dad, ran upstairs, and hopped in the shower.

He'd had lots of messy days this summer. Most of these were because of the Stermont Summer Maker Program. He often came home from camp covered in marker, paint, glue, or even glitter.

I can't wait to find out what this week's project will be! he thought as the last of the soapy water swirled around the drain.

He stepped out of the shower. Then, even though the bathroom was steamy, he shivered —

Two eyes stared at him from the foggy bathroom mirror. Angry, evil eyes.

Alexander wiped the mirror and saw his own eyes looking back, wide with fear.

He grabbed his toothbrush and ran downstairs.

"Al?" his dad asked. "Why are you brushing your teeth over the kitchen sink?"

Alexander wanted to say, "Because there's no mirror down here with foggy monster eyes in it!"

But he didn't say anything because grown-ups couldn't see monsters.

Instead, he just mumbled with a mouthful of toothpaste and spat in the sink.

SOGGY SOCKS

"**S**low down, Al!" said Alexander's dad at breakfast. "You're getting syrup everywhere!"

Alexander swallowed his last bite of pancake. "Sorry! I'm meeting Rip and Nikki before camp."

"Oh … sounds important!" said his dad, smiling. "Then you'd better skedaddle! Don't forget your shoes are still out on the porch."

Alexander hugged his dad and ran outside.

He blinked. The porch was totally clean — not a single smudge of mud anywhere. Even his sneakers sparkled in the sunlight.

Nice! thought Alexander. *Dad must have cleaned everything up last night. I'll have to thank him later.*

He stuck a foot in one sneaker. **SQUISH!** The shoe was totally wet.

"Dang!" said Alexander.

He thought about running inside to find another pair of shoes. *Forget it!* he decided. *A monster meeting is more important than having dry feet!*

SQUISH! He put on his other shoe. Then he raced downtown on his bike.

He parked and snuck into the woods behind the library.

Nine hundred squishy footsteps later, he arrived at the S.S.M.P. headquarters.

Three stories tall!

Slides for going down.

Ladders for going up.

Rip and Nikki were swinging on an oversized tire swing.

"Hop on, Salamander!" Nikki called.

Alexander climbed on the swing. "I saw a monster last night!" he said.

"Really?!" asked Rip. "Did it have tentacles? Or a stinger? Or six rows of teeth?"

"Um, I'm not sure," said Alexander. "I just saw two eyes. In my bathroom mirror."

"What kind of eyes?" asked Nikki.

"They looked . . . evil," said Alexander. "And um, foggy. But when I wiped the mirror, they were gone."

"Hmm," said Nikki. "Then maybe you didn't see a monster."

Alexander leaned back, pulling hard on the swing's rope as he tried to remember the eyes. That's when he spotted something in the tire — a bit of paper.

"Is that what I think it is?" he asked.

The swing came to a halt as Alexander grabbed the paper.

"It's a monster card!" Rip said.

SPLATTER-PILLAR

LEVEL 4

A greasy bug that sprays gunk on your lunch.

ATTACKS	SLIME-SPURT!	40	GOO-SPEW!	30

HABITAT

Sticky, drippy cocoon.

DIET

 Wilted lettuce, drizzled with spoiled mayo.

TYPE

BUG

GROSS

In late spring, this monster transforms into a sputter-fly.

Alexander took a binder from his backpack. He flipped past pages of maps and drawings to a section filled with monster cards. Then he added this new card to the binder.

"I wish we knew who was leaving these cards everywhere," said Rip.

"Yeah," said Nikki. "It's weird how we're always finding them in places where we hang out."

"Maybe it's the evil-eye monster," said Alexander. "Maybe it's hiding these cards just for us to find."

"Maaaaybe . . ." said Rip. "If you really did see a monster in the mirror."

"I did!" said Alexander. "I'm almost definitely ninety-nine percent kinda-sorta sure!"

Alexander hopped down from the swing and looked at his friends. "Okay, fine. I don't know what I saw. Let's just get to maker-camp."

PUDDLE JUMPER

Alexander, Rip, and Nikki were walking out of the woods when Alexander froze in his tracks.

"Listen!" he said. "Do you hear something?"

His friends paused.

CLACK! SKITTER! CLOMP-CLOMP-CLOMP!

"It's coming from the front of the library," said Rip.

"It sounds like a rock rolling down the sidewalk," said Nikki. "And somebody jumping, maybe?"

"It must be the evil-eye monster!" said Alexander. He peeked around the side of the building.

"Hi, Alexander!" shouted a friendly voice.

"That doesn't sound like a monster," said Rip. He and Nikki laughed as they ran around front. Alexander followed.

Three kids from camp were playing on the sidewalk. Becka was drawing squares with chalk. Chuck was writing numbers inside each square. And May was standing on one foot, holding a stone in her hand.

CLACK! SKITTER! May tossed her stone onto one of the boxes. **CLOMP-CLOMP-CLOMP!** She hopped along, avoiding the square with the stone.

"We're playing hopscotch," said Chuck.

"Try it! It's fun!" said Becka.

Rip and Nikki hopped along the hopscotch court.

"Your turn, Alexander!" said May.

"Do it with your eyes closed!" added Rip.

Alexander stepped up to the first square and tossed his stone. Then he closed his eyes and started hopping.

CLOMP-CLOMP! CLOMP-CLOMP! CLOMP-CLOMP! SPLASH!

"Dang!" said Alexander, opening his eyes. He had landed in a big puddle past square number 10.

"Ha!" said Rip. "Only *you* could land in a puddle on a sunny day!"

Alexander sighed as he followed the rest of the campers into the library.

CHAPTER 4

COOLEST, NEATEST, BEST-EST

The campers plopped down on beanbags. The library was warm, sunny, and fun. Just like the librarian.

"Good morning, maker-bees!" said Ms. Sprinkles. She circled the beanbags, high-fiving each camper. "Get ready for the coolest, neatest challenge of the summer! This week, we're going to tackle some world records!"

She brought out a large book.

The campers spent the next several minutes pointing at photos of people doing incredible tricks and stunts.

"Gross!" said Chuck. "That guy's covered in worms!"

"That girl's playing four recorders — with her nose!" said Becka.

"Check out that motorcycle-riding axe-juggler!" said Rip.

"Those world records are all really fun," Ms. Sprinkles said. "But this week, our town is going to break the best-est world record ever!"

Ms. Sprinkles pointed to a poster on the wall.

Gather 'round the bonfire for
S'MORE-FEST!

The town of Stermont will make history by creating
THE WORLD'S BIGGEST S'MORE!

GIGANTIC
GRAHAM CRACKERS
provided by Crumb Brothers Bakery.

MASSIVE
MARSHMALLOW
provided by Stermont Sweet Shop.

TONS OF
CHOCOLATE
provided by YOU!
Everyone attending should
bring chocolate bars to
add to the s'more.

WHEN: Wednesday at sunset.
WHERE: The Stermont Bowl, in Derwood Park.

(Sponsored by Stermont Realty.)

"S'more-Fest is going to be a big deal," said Ms. Sprinkles. "Even the mayor will be there! So to get in the spirit, you're each going to set your *own* world record on Wednesday!"

She wheeled over the whiteboard.

THIS WEEK'S MAKER-CHALLENGE

TODAY & TONIGHT: Read about world records to get ideas for your own!

TOMORROW: Come ready with your idea. Then get to work breaking that record!

WEDNESDAY: Share time! Show us your work.

WEDNESDAY NIGHT: S'more-Fest at the park!

The campers flipped through books, looking for inspiration.

"I wish there were a record for *most monsters defeated*," Nikki whispered to Alexander and Rip.

"Yeah, we'd break that one, easily!" Rip laughed.

But Alexander wasn't listening. He was too busy sketching in his binder. There was only one monster he wanted to find now.

DIRTY WORDS

Alexander, Rip, and Nikki compared world-record books on their walk home.

"I bet I could do the longest hula-hoop session while eating vanilla pudding," said Rip.

"No way," said Nikki. "The record is fourteen hours, nine minutes."

"How about butterscotch?" said Rip.

BEEP-BEEEEP!

The three friends looked up as Alexander's dad pulled over.

"Hey, kiddos!" he said, waving. "I'm off to get the car washed. I didn't realize how dirty it had gotten until someone left me a message!"

Alexander looked at the car. It was covered in dust and grime. Along the side, someone had written:

Alexander, Rip, and Nikki looked at the large, splashy letters.

"It's a warning!" Alexander whispered.

"Nah," said Rip. "It's probably just a prank."

"Rip's right," said Nikki. "People write 'wash me' on dirty cars all the time."

"Hop in, you three," said Alexander's dad. "I'll drive you home after we give the Bopp-mobile a good scrubbing!"

Alexander climbed in and scooched over to make room for his friends. Then he paused.

There, tucked under the seat belt, was another monster card.

BITE-BULB

An 800-watt monster who's a bit dim.

ATTACKS **FLASH-BASH!** **10** **SOCKET-SOCK!** **15**

HABITAT

Lamps, closets, and the basement stairway.

DIET

Electric eels.

TYPE

THINGY

BUG

 This monster likes to appear over your head. Not a good idea.

The S.S.M.P. whispered while Alexander's dad drove.

"The bite-bulb sure looks freaky," said Rip.

"Is that the monster you saw, Salamander?" asked Nikki.

"It can't be," said Alexander. "The bite-bulb has eight eyes, but I only saw two in my bathroom mirror."

"Kids, look!" said Alexander's dad from the front seat. "The town is getting ready for S'more-Fest!"

They were driving by the park, where workers were stacking logs for a huge bonfire.

WASH ME. OR ELSE!

A few minutes later, Alexander's dad pulled into the Stermont Auto Wash.

The outside of the building was bright and cheery, but the inside was dark and steamy.

"It looks like we're about to drive into a giant, hungry mouth," whispered Alexander.

He, Rip, and Nikki swallowed as the car rolled inside.

ALL WASHED UP

Alexander looked out the grimy front windshield as the car entered the deep, dark car wash.

PWSSSHHHH! Sprayers splashed the hood.

FLAM-FLAM-FLAM! Wriggling raggedy-noodles slapped against the windshield.

Alexander tilted his head. He could hear something — a hissing, gurgling sound — beneath the sound of the sprayers and the noodles.

Alexander gulped.

The hissing gurgle was a voice! **"YOU WILL BE CLEAN!"** it said.

Alexander looked at Rip and Nikki. "Did you hear that?" he whispered.

They nodded, their eyes as big as headlights.

"Yeah!" his dad shouted from the front seat. "Those spray-jets sure are loud!"

FWOOOSHH! Clouds of steam filled the tunnel as jets blasted the car with hot, sudsy water.

VWIRRR! Scrubber-arms came down from the ceiling, whirring like power drills.

Alexander gasped. For a brief moment, he saw something wet and shiny bobbing behind the scrubbers. It looked like some sort of animal with a snout.

"Is that . . . an alligator?" he whispered. The steam was so thick Alexander could barely see out the window.

"No!" said Rip. "It's got a long neck . . ."

"Like a dragon!" added Nikki.

Alexander, Rip, and Nikki huddled together as the car rocked and lurched from the force of the scrubbers.

"Yee-haw!" shouted Alexander's dad. "This is like an amusement park ride!"

GLORRRGGHHH! With a gut-turning gurgle, a monstrous face rose up behind the car.

"Ack!" said Nikki. "The dragon-gator is behind us!"

"It looks more like a bird!" said Rip. "That's a beak, not a snout!"

The sudsy monster reared back and — **WHAM!** It smashed against the car.

Then, with a final slurping sound, the monster disappeared.

FWUMMMMM! A powerful blower swung down, blasting the car with hot air. Alexander could feel the heat from inside the car, which became dry in seconds.

Alexander's dad whistled as he drove out into the sunlight. "Our car is spotless!" he said. "It's shinier than a molar after a six-month checkup!" Then he sang along with the radio.

Alexander looked back at the Stermont Auto Wash. There was no sign of a soapy, dancing, long-necked alligator-dragon-bird.

"What was that thing?" asked Nikki.

"Beats me!" said Rip. "It was hard to see in there!"

"I did make out one important detail," said Alexander. "It had the same evil eyes I saw in my bathroom mirror."

Rip's and Nikki's mouths fell open.

EVIL RAINBOW

Alexander thought about the evil-eye monster all night. And during breakfast the next morning. And on his ride to maker-camp.

He was *so* focused on the monster, he almost didn't see the fire truck in front of the library.

SKKRRRRRT! Alexander slammed on the brakes, dropped his bike, and ran up the wet sidewalk. A firefighter was talking to Ms. Sprinkles and the campers.

He read the patch on the firefighter's suit.

"We've been seeing puddles like this everywhere," said Chief Teresa. "We think some prankster has been opening fire hydrants all over town."

"That prankster washed away our hopscotch court!" said May.

Alexander looked down. The sidewalk was totally clean — there was no trace of the hopscotch court.

"Cheer up!" said Becka. "I brought treats!" She opened a cooler and handed out ice pops. "I need you to eat them so I can use the sticks for my project."

Everyone took an ice pop except for Rip. "Uh, sugar doesn't exactly agree with me," he said, giving Alexander and Nikki a look.

Chief Teresa chose a lemon ice pop. "The weird part is, the hydrants are all closed when I get to them," she said. "Anyhow, I've got to check on a couple more puddles over at the park. I've got to make sure everything's ship-shape for S'more-Fest!"

The campers waved with drippy, sticky hands as Chief Teresa drove away.

"Oops!" said Ms. Sprinkles. "Looks like those ice pops were a bit melty." She turned to Alexander. "Would you grab that garden hose so we can rinse off before we head inside?"

"Sure!" said Alexander. He jogged across the lawn and picked up the hose.

"Ow!" he said. The hose felt hot from lying in the sun.

Alexander twisted the nozzle.
At first, nothing happened.
Then the hose began to shake.

A second later: **SPLISH!** Water sprayed upward. Alexander could see a rainbow where the water hit the sunlight. And then, Alexander saw two evil eyes.

"Ack!" He threw down the hose. It flopped and flailed like an angry snake, gushing water.

Everyone was drenched from head to toe. Actually, not everyone. Alexander was perfectly dry.

CHAPTER 8

CHALK ON THE WALK

"**A**ll right, maker-bees!" said Ms. Sprinkles. "We will have camp outside today so we can dry off. Let's start by sharing our world-record ideas."

The campers showed their plans.

Becka: Tallest ice-pop-stick skyscraper.

Nikki: Fruitiest salsa.

Alexander: Biggest macaroni sculpture.

Chuck and May: Longest hopscotch course.

Rip: Hugest-ever bubble-gum bubble.

Ms. Sprinkles smiled at Rip. "Do you think you can blow a bubble *that* big?"

"MRGHM-GRMM-GRHMM!" said Rip. He pulled an enormous wad of gum from his mouth. "I'm an expert on blowing bubbles! I even wrote up a gum guide last night!"

He handed a sheet of paper to Ms. Sprinkles.

RIP'S POP-TASTIC GUIDE TO GUM!

HISTORY

Long ago, in the days before gum, people would chew all kinds of stuff, like sap, wax and even tar.

Then, one day — POP! — gum came along.

NYAM NYAM!

The first gum tasted like spice and licorice.

But in the 1920s, factories finally made actual, delicious, stick-to-your-face bubble gum!

PRO TIP:
Only chew sugar-free gum. Too much sugar can turn you into a real monster!

WHY DO PEOPLE CHEW GUM?

13%

9%

73%

5%

Clean breath. Winter fresh!

Jaw strength. Moo! That kid can chew!

To annoy principals. My office. Now.

To plug a leaky ship. Ahoy!

HOW TO BLOW HUGE BUBBLES

1 Chew your gum until it's just right.

TOO STIFF!

NO FLAVOR!

JUST RIGHT!

2 Take a deeeeep breath, like you're about to dive for sunken treasure.

3 Moosh your tongue against the gum and BLOW!

HOW DID YOU DO?

ping-pong ball-size bubble

🎖 Bronze

basketball-size bubble

🎖 Silver

boulder-size bubble

🏆 WORLD RECORD!

Ms. Sprinkles read Rip's comic in a serious voice, like a TV newscaster. Everyone laughed. "Terrific ideas, maker-bees," she said. "Now let's grab our chalk, bubble gum, hot peppers, and art supplies, and get started!"

Then the campers went to work.

"I'm still bummed our original hopscotch court got washed away," said Chuck. "But this clean sidewalk is like a big blank sheet of paper!"

Alexander looked around. The sidewalk really was clean. And so were the streets. And the buildings. Even the trash cans sparkled in the sunlight.

Downtown looks as clean as Dad's car, thought Alexander. *And my front porch . . .*

"Let's get to work!" said May.

They worked all morning and part of the afternoon, only taking a break for lunch.

By early afternoon, Alexander was covered in glue, paint, and macaroni. And so was his sculpture.

"Ooh, scary!" said Ms. Sprinkles. Then she called the other campers over. "Come see, maker-bees! We can admire how Alexander's macaroni sculpture is coming along while we try Nikki's salsa."

Nikki passed around cups of salsa. Everyone grabbed a chip, dipped it, and took a bite.

"YEOW!" they all shouted.

Three campers dropped their cups, splattering salsa on the sidewalk.

Everyone ran inside to drink from the water fountain.

Ms. Sprinkles had tears in her eyes. "Whew! That's spicy!" she said to Nikki. "I think you just broke the record for hottest salsa!"

"Oops! I must've used too many peppers," said Nikki. "I'll go find a cookbook and double-check the recipe."

The rest of the campers headed back outside.

"How's your bubble-blowing going, Rip?" Alexander asked.

"It's tricky," said Rip. "If I blow too hard, my gum goes flying all over the —"

SPLISH!

Rip had stepped in a puddle. "Ugh!" he groaned. "Where did that come from?"

Alexander looked around. Once again, the sidewalk was wet. The spilled salsa was gone. And so was the hopscotch court. His macaroni sculpture was still standing, but all the spilled glue, glitter, and macaroni had been washed away.

"Not again!" said Chuck.

Alexander pulled Rip aside. "There's not a cloud in the sky. What kind of monster did all this?" he whispered.

"Monster?" asked Rip. "You heard the firefighter. It was probably that same prankster who's been opening fire hydrants."

Nikki burst out the door. "Look what I found in this cookbook!"

Alexander was still sweating from the salsa, but he felt a chill as Nikki handed him another monster card.

OWL-A-PEÑO

Fire-breathing bird whoooo lights up the night.

| ATTACKS | HOT-HOOT! | 30 | FLAME-FLAP! | 70 |

HABITAT

Trees with reddish-orange leaves, to match its feathers.

DIET

Hot stuff! (Peppers, lava, fireworks.)

TYPE

CRITTER

UNKNOWN

A well-fed owl-a-peño can burn an entire city.

CHAPTER 9

RED-HOT CLUES

The minute maker-camp was over, Alexander, Rip, and Nikki ran to their S.S.M.P. headquarters to review monster clues.

"The monster causing all this trouble *must* be an owl-a-peño!" said Nikki.

POP! Rip snapped his gum. "The flaming-owl monster?"

"Yes!" said Alexander. "Look at the card — it loves hot stuff! I bet it was drawn to the hot steam in my bathroom."

"And we saw it at the hottest car wash in town!" added Rip.

"Plus, that rubber hose I picked up was super hot . . ." said Alexander. "And that was right before I saw the evil eyes!" He squinted at the card. "But these eyes don't look exactly like the evil eyes from my mirror or from the car wash."

"The car wash was too steamy," said Rip. "It was hard to tell *what* we saw in there!"

"And remember — my hot salsa vanished this afternoon!" cried Nikki. "The owl-a-peño must have swooped in for a snack! The card says it eats hot stuff."

Alexander scribbled some notes in his binder.

hot bathroom
hot car wash
+ hot salsa
OWL-A-PEÑO!

"Oh, nooooo," said Nikki, rereading the monster card. "The owl-a-peño has fire-powers! It could burn down the whole town!"

"If this birdbrain has fire-powers, we can stop it with water!" said Rip.

Alexander thought for a moment. "But its weakness *can't* be water," he said. "Because we keep seeing it around wet stuff."

"That's true. Well . . . what else fights fire?" asked Rip.

"Ice!" shouted Nikki. "We could stop it with ice!"

"Good thinking!" said Alexander. "Maybe we can freeze it."

"What if we trap it in Becka's ice-pop cooler?" asked Nikki.

"It probably wouldn't fit," said Rip. "We should trap it in an ice-cream truck!"

"Where would we find an ice-cream truck?" asked Alexander. "How about this: We'll brainstorm at home and make a plan in the morning. Just stay away from anything hot tonight!"

Alexander scanned the sky as he walked home. He saw a bright red sunset, but no flaming-hot owls.

To be safe, he convinced his dad to have a cold dinner.

"I can't wait for S'more-Fest tomorrow!" said Alexander's dad. He handed Alexander a chocolate bar. "Here — this is for the giant s'more! I just hope everyone brushes their teeth after they chomp on that humongous marshmallow."

Alexander laughed, and headed up to bed.

He listened for hoots as he drifted off to sleep, but heard nothing.

He smiled and slept soundly, confident he was one step ahead of the monster.

Unfortunately, he was wrong.

RECORD BREAKERS

The next morning was hot and sunshiny. *A perfect day for a bike ride to the library*, thought Alexander.

Then he frowned as sweat dripped down his forehead. It was also a perfect day for a flaming-owl creature who draws its power from heat.

He passed Derwood Park. Workers were building a metal arch over a log pile.

STERMONT BOWL

When Alexander got to the library, he found everyone working on their world records outside, near the fountain. Rip was pumping himself up for his giant bubble.

Biggest bubble

Tallest tower

Becka's ice-pop-stick tower was taller than she was. Nikki was mixing a huge bowl of salsa.

Fruitiest salsa

Longest course

And May and Chuck were drawing their third hopscotch court of the week.

Alexander waved to Rip and Nikki. They raced right over.

POP! Rip snapped his gum. "We came up with the perfect plan to trap the owl-a-peño!"

He snatched up a piece of chalk and drew on the sidewalk.

OPERATION BRRRR:

1. BAIT!
Nikki mixes up an extra-hot batch of ten-alarm salsa.

2. WAIT!
We hang out behind the library, listening for hoots.

3. BREEZY!
The owl-a-peño swoops in to eat!

4. FREEZY!
The S.S.M.P smacks the monster with a flurry of ice pops!

"Great plan!" said Alexander. "So the bait is already out. Now we wait."

"Keep an eye on the sky as we work on our world records," Nikki added.

The S.S.M.P. went about their day. Rip and Nikki hung out near the fountain, while Alexander got busy with macaroni, glitter, and googly-eyes.

Yum's

Free

HOTTEST
salsa

507
506
504 505
503
501 502
500
498 499
497

Before they knew it, the
afternoon had arrived, and there
was still no sign of the owl-a-peño.
"Maker-bees, gather around!" called
Ms. Sprinkles. "It's share-time! I can't wait to
hear how you each set a record!"

The campers showed off their work.

"Wonderful!" said Ms. Sprinkles. "I love seeing
all this creativity!"

Then she frowned a tiny bit. "None of you made it into the official world-record book ... but you all made it into *this* book!"

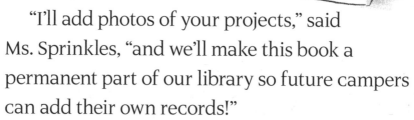

Her smile came back as she held up a large, colorful, homemade book.

"I'll add photos of your projects," said Ms. Sprinkles, "and we'll make this book a permanent part of our library so future campers can add their own records!"

The campers cheered.

"I can tell you worked hard, because you're all so messy," said Ms. Sprinkles.

The campers looked at one another, and laughed.

"Now, head home to clean up!" said Ms. Sprinkles. "S'more-Fest starts at sunset tonight!"

But the three friends did not run straight home. They walked over to Nikki's giant bowl of extra-spicy salsa on the ground.

"I don't get it," said Rip. "Why didn't hooty hot-wings take the bait?"

"Well, the owl-a-peño already tried my salsa yesterday," said Nikki. "Maybe it's hungry for something hotter."

Alexander gasped. "Of course!" he said. He walked over to a S'more-Fest poster and jabbed his finger at the glowing red bonfire.

"Let's race home and gear up," Alexander continued. "Find anything you can that's ice-cold. We'll meet at the park just before sunset."

S'MORE-
FEST!

□ + ▬ + ▨

TONIGHT!

CHAPTER 11

THE BONFIRE

It was almost sunset when Alexander met Rip and Nikki at Derwood Park. Townspeople were spilling in from all sides.

"Did you bring cold stuff?" asked Alexander.

"Yep!" said Rip. "I tried to freeze some water balloons!" He held up a bulging bag. "They're a little slushy, but still cold!"

"And I filled this soak-blaster with chilled strawberry smoothie!" said Nikki.

"Awesome," said Alexander. "All I found was this ice-pack from when I scraped my knee last summer."

BEEP-BEEP-BEEP! A bakery truck backed up. Two workers hauled out sheets of what looked like plywood.

"Whoa!" said Nikki. "Those are GIANT graham crackers!"

"There you are!" said Alexander's dad, jogging over. "Come on! Let's add our chocolate bars to the s'more!"

Alexander and his friends unwrapped their chocolate bars and stacked them onto the oversized graham crackers. Then they followed the townspeople down a hill to a low, grassy area.

"I see why they call this part of the park the Stermont Bowl," said Nikki.

STERMONT
BOWL
CAUTION!
STEEP INCLINE!

60

A towering woodpile sat in the middle
of the clearing. A metal arch was built over
the woodpile. Hanging from the arch was an
enormous marshmallow the size of a refrigerator.

"Neat-o!" said Alexander's dad, pointing to a banner. "That's how they're going to make the s'more!"

WORLD'S BIGGEST SMORE!

PULL LEVER TO RELEASE MARSHMALLOW!

"Who cares how they make it?" said Rip. "I can't wait to *eat* it!"

Alexander looked around. He saw Becka, May, and Chuck with their families. He saw Chief Teresa. He saw Ms. Sprinkles. But he didn't see a fire-breathing owl.

"We haven't heard a single hoot!" said Rip.

"Or seen a single flaming feather!" said Nikki.

"I bet the owl-a-peño's waiting for the bonfire to get fired up," said Alexander.

"Shhh!" said Alexander's dad. "Mayor Shank is about to speak!"

A man in suspenders stepped up to the woodpile. "Citizens of Stermont!" said the mayor. "We're going to make history tonight!"

The crowd cheered.

"I'd like to thank Stermont Sweet Shop for this magnificent marshmallow, and Crumb Brothers Bakery for these colossal crackers. I'd also like to thank all of *you* for bringing in seventeen hundred chocolate bars."

The crowd cheered louder.

"This s'more will not only break the world record," said Mayor Shank. "It'll break the hearts of every other mayor who wishes *they* had thought of such a cool idea! This s'more will put Stermont on the map!"

MARSHMALLOW RELEASE

The mayor held a small torch above the woodpile.

"Get ready," Alexander whispered to his friends. He adjusted his grip on his ice-pack. Rip held a slush-balloon in each hand. And Nikki gave her smoothie-blaster an extra pump.

The mayor dropped the torch.

FWOOOM! The bonfire burst into flames.

Right beside the bonfire, the chocolate bars began to melt on the stack of giant crackers.

The fire roared. So did the crowd.

"Things are heating up now!" said Alexander.

The three friends strained to listen for a hoot.

The huge marshmallow began to get toasty on the bottom. So did Alexander. He took a step back.

SPLISH! He felt a familiar sensation. For the third time this week, his shoes were wet.

Alexander, Rip, and Nikki all looked down.

A gush of water was streaming across the ground, straight toward the bonfire.

A SPLASHY ENTRANCE

Rip stomped in a large puddle that was quickly becoming a pool. "What the heck?!" he shouted. "Where's all this water coming from?"

"The park is flooding!" said Nikki, hopping onto a park bench.

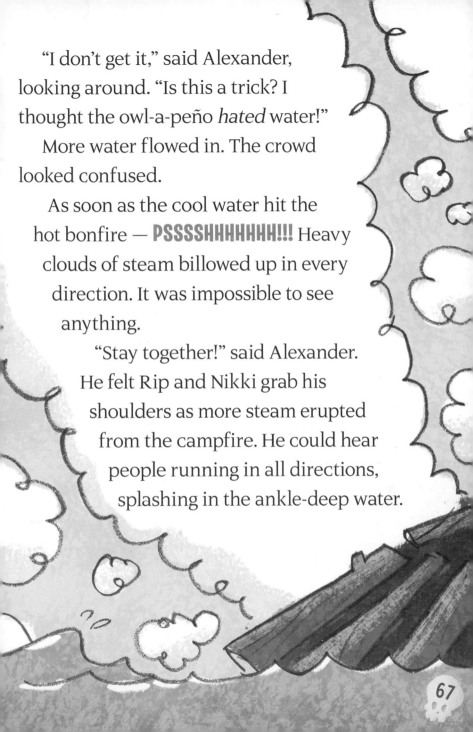

"I don't get it," said Alexander, looking around. "Is this a trick? I thought the owl-a-peño *hated* water!"

More water flowed in. The crowd looked confused.

As soon as the cool water hit the hot bonfire — **PSSSSHHHHHHH!!!** Heavy clouds of steam billowed up in every direction. It was impossible to see anything.

"Stay together!" said Alexander. He felt Rip and Nikki grab his shoulders as more steam erupted from the campfire. He could hear people running in all directions, splashing in the ankle-deep water.

Then he heard Mayor Shank's voice over a loudspeaker. "Everyone: The Stermont Bowl is flooding! S'more-Fest is canceled! Please remain calm, but also, get out of here!"

"Rats!" said Alexander's dad. "You kids run to your bikes. Al, I'll see you back at home."

Everyone splashed toward the park exit.

Everyone except Alexander, Rip, and Nikki. They turned to face the bonfire. Or what was left of it. A few embers glowed orange, and then died. For a few seconds, the water was still and the park was quiet.

But then —

SPLISH-SPLISH-SPLISH!

"I hear footsteps!" said Rip. "Something's running this way!"

Alexander peered into the steam. He saw a flash of red. A small creature splashed through the still-rising water and hopped onto the soggy woodpile.

"It's the monster!" said Alexander. "ATTACK!" The three friends raised their slush-balloons, smoothie-blaster, and ice-pack. Then they charged into the steam.

WATER *YOU* DOING HERE?

The Super Secret Monster Patrol splashed toward the monster, bombarding it with their icy gear.

"Take that, you fire-breathing feather-ball!" said Rip, snapping his gum.

The steam cloud began to clear.

"Did we get it?" asked Alexander. "Did we stop the fire-monster?"

"Nope!" A strange, echoey voice spoke from the steam. **"I'm not a fire-monster. I am a water-monster! You filthy blockheads got it all wrong!"**

"Huh?!" said Nikki.

As the last of the steam faded away, Alexander's jaw dropped. So did Nikki's. Rip's would have, too, if he hadn't been blowing a huge bubble.

The monster on the soggy woodpile wasn't an owl-a-peño. It was an angry fire hydrant. One of its valves was open and gushing water.

BLOP! Rip's bubble burst. His face was covered in gum.

"Glugh!" The hydrant made a gurgly groan. *"Look at you messy kids, with your glitter and your sidewalk chalk and your gum!"*

BLOOSH! The hydrant blasted water onto Rip's gum-covered face.

SPLOP! Rip fell back into the rising water. The gum was washed away.

"Much better!" said the hydrant. *"The grown-ups in Stermont should be thanking me for cleaning up after their disgusting kids! Your messes make me so steamed-up I could spout!"*

The hydrant popped another valve, and started gushing water twice as fast.

The water was now up to Alexander's chin, and rising fast.

"Go for higher ground!" Alexander shouted to his friends. "It's the only — blurble-blurb!" He couldn't finish his sentence. He was in over his head.

STAYING AFLOAT

Alexander held his breath and looked up. He was underwater — the park was now more like a lake. He could see the moon up there, glowing white against the night sky. Wait, it wasn't the moon — it was the hot, goopy, two-ton marshmallow! He kicked to the surface and grabbed on to a log drifting by.

"There you are, you little squirt!" said the hydrant.

The monster hopped onto Alexander's log. It leaned down, pressing its cold, metal nose-bolt into Alexander's face. *"I tried to scare you into staying clean — in the mirror and in the car wash,"* the hydrant gurgled, *"but you just keep —"*

BLORP! A glop of something brown splatted against the hydrant's face.

"Gah!" The hydrant jumped. *"Chocolate?! Get-it-off-get-it-off-get-it-off!"*

"Dry up, nozzle-nose!" shouted Rip.

Alexander turned to see Rip and Nikki standing on a raft, lobbing handfuls of melted chocolate at the hydrant.

Actually, it wasn't a raft. It was a stack of giant graham crackers.

"NOBODY makes ME dirty! You slobby kids are always tracking in mud, spilling salsa, and ruining sidewalks with your terrible artwork!" the monster shouted. *"I'm going to flood this entire town to clean it from top to bottom. But first: I'll wash YOU away!"*

The hydrant blasted up into the air, like a water-powered jet. It popped its top and spun in the sky, gushing water like an oversized lawn sprinkler.

Water drops stung Alexander's face as he swam over to Rip and Nikki. They pulled him onto the stack of crackers and melted chocolate.

"Let's get to dry land!" said Nikki. She leaned over the edge of the cracker-raft and began paddling.

"We need all the help we can get," said Rip. He made three loud clicks with his tongue. A few ants hopped from his pocket and gave him a little salute.

"Eat up, mateys!" said Rip.

The ants nibbled at the chocolate. **BA-DINK!** They transformed into gi-norm-ants, and began to paddle the raft with swift, six-legged strokes.

"Yes! We're getting away!" said Alexander.

"Not for long!" rang out a voice from above.

The hydrant jetted toward the S.S.M.P.'s raft, water-cannons blasting.

CRACKING UP

GALOOSH!

A hundred gallons of water hit the S.S.M.P.'s raft. It began to crumble apart.

"I'll dunk you all!" shouted the hydrant.

"It's time to fight fire with fire!" said Rip. "I mean, to fight water with, um, me. You know what I mean." He leaned down and took a bite from the chocolatey raft.

 **RAWWWR!** Rip transformed into the knuckle-fisted punch-smasher.

With a roar, monster-Rip leaped from the raft, straight toward the fireplug.

CLANG! Rip head-butted the tiny hydrant. For a moment, they both hung in the air.

KRRRICK! A deep crack ran up the hydrant's metal body. The monster frowned as its powerful gush of water slowed to a trickle.

PLOP! Monster-Rip dropped into the lake.

Regular-Rip surfaced.

"You did it!" cheered Alexander. He and Nikki pulled Rip aboard what was left of their raft.

"You stopped the monster!" said Nikki.

The hydrant began to shake. Then it laughed, dribbling water. **"You haven't stopped me! You've only cracked my armor. Let's see how you dirt-trackers handle my true form! Bow down to the HYDRANT-HYDRA!"**

The monster's red metal shell fell away. In its place, a massive water creature rose up. It had a dragon-like snout and the same evil eyes Alexander had been seeing all week.

BLOOP! The water level lowered slightly as three more hydra-heads rose from the surface.

"Whoa!" said Nikki. "That's a lot of heads!"

"We're surrounded!" said Alexander.

THAT'S S'MORE LIKE IT

Alexander, Rip, and Nikki huddled on their crumbling cracker as the hydrant-hydra let out a four-headed roar.

"How can we stop a monster made of water?" asked Nikki.

Alexander looked around. He could see the tops of trees and the tall metal arch. The melty marshmallow still hung from the arch, just above the water's surface.

The monster's heads zeroed in on the cracker-raft. Then — **BLOOP!** — a fifth head rose from the surface, and **BLOOP!** A sixth. With each new head, the water level got a little lower.

"Crud!" said Rip. "How many heads can this monster make?"

The largest hydra-head flashed Rip an evil grin. **"AS MANY AS I LIKE!"** it gurgled.

A dozen more watery heads rose up. The lake lowered a few more feet.

Alexander gasped. Then he smiled, slightly.

"We give up!" he shouted to the hydra. "Just please, stop growing more heads!"

"Huh?!" said Rip.

"YOU WISH!" roared the monster's heads, all at once.

FWOOOSH!

The hydrant-hydra sucked up every last drop of water in the park, growing larger and twisting itself into a giant, *living* wave.

The S.S.M.P. and the crumbly bits of their raft plopped down into the mud.

The hydra-wave rippled with anger. **"JUST LOOK AT THIS MESS!"** it roared.

Alexander looked down at the mud, the soggy cracker bits, and the gobs of chocolate. Then he looked up at the huge, drippy marshmallow.

"You think we're messy *now?*" Alexander shouted. "We're just getting started!"

He turned to Rip and Nikki. "Follow my lead, *swamp* creatures!"

Alexander, Rip, and Nikki flopped about, covering themselves in muck.

"THAT'S THE LAST SMUDGE!" the monster gurgled. **"PREPARE FOR THE ULTIMATE BATH!"**

The monster-wave launched itself into the air. It swirled around, compressing itself into an angry-looking, two-ton raindrop.

Alexander reached into Rip's muddy bag and grabbed the last slush-balloon.

"We've got one shot," he said to Nikki, passing her the balloon. "Hit that lever!"

As the giant raindrop flew down, Nikki lobbed Rip's balloon at the lever.

BLOOSH!

MARSHMALLOW RELEASE

BLOP!

The drop plopped on the S.S.M.P.

FLOMP! . . . followed by the massive marshmallow . . .

WHAM! . . . and a gigantic graham cracker.

The world's largest s'more sat in the middle of the mud pit. Alexander, Rip, Nikki, and the hydrant-hydra were trapped between layers of marshmallow and chocolate.

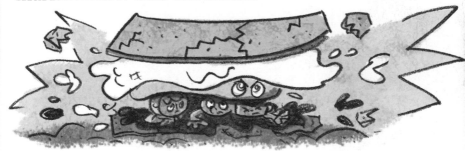

Just then, the s'more began to tremble. And crack. The gooey, heavy marshmallow smooshed down on the three friends — and on the monster!

"What's . . . happening . . . to . . . me?"
the monster gurgled. "I'm so . . . messy . . ."
Then —

KER-PLOWIE!!!

The s'more exploded.

Globs of wet marshmallow, chocolate, and
cracker splatted into the mud. So did Alexander,
Rip, and Nikki.

"What happened to that oversized drip?"
asked Rip, looking around.

"I guess it couldn't handle getting turned into
a super-sized s'more," said Nikki.

"The hydrant-hydra was more mess than
monster in the end," said Alexander.

"Ha!" said Rip. He gave Alexander a friendly
slap on the back. "Oh — Salamander!
Something is stuck to your shirt!"

HYDRANT-HYDRA

LEVEL 4

World's cleanest monster.

ATTACKS | **GALLON-GALOOSH!** 20 | **DRIPPY-DUNK!** 30

HABITAT

Any place with plumbing: car washes, bathrooms, etc.

DIET

Grapefruit-scented soap.

TYPE

THINGY

UNKNOWN

The hydrant-hydra's many-headed body can transform into a giant wave or a dense raindrop.

"I can't believe we thought this thing was a fiery owl monster!" said Alexander.

Rip nodded. "But if an owl-a-peño ever *does* show up, I've got fifty more water balloons in my freezer!"

Nikki looked over at the muddy glob of what used to be the hydrant-hydra. "Nobody will know we actually made the world's largest s'more, after all. But we did break another record! We just made the world's largest *mud pie*!"

Alexander laughed as he put his sticky, gloppy arms around his friends' shoulders. "Right now, the only record I want to break is: WORLD'S LONGEST SHOWER."